Cover design and illustrations by Patrick N. Marston

Paperback ISBN-13:978-0-9600783-3-2

eBook ISBN-13:

Library of Congress Control Number:2019907716

DEDICATION

Jessica – *To my awesome writing partners, Tabitha and Patrick! You guys are making my dreams come true! For Chris, who makes me ceaselessly happy. And to my fur babies, who make my life so fun and chaotic. Momma loves you, Tank, Nymeria and Heimdallr. Love to Doggy Heaven for Oy, Finnick and Sookie Bear. We miss you.*

Tabitha – *To Jessica and Patrick, may all the work we do put a twinkle to your eye, smile on your face and warmth in your heart. Thank you for your creativity, hard work and dedication.*

Patrick – *To Jessica, Tabitha, my two Scotties, and especially my wife. Thank you for the patience and support!*

SCOOTER STEALS THE BALL

By **TJ Trumar**

Illustrated by Patrick N. Marston

It was a bright, sunny day and everyone was excited. It was the first baseball game of the season.

The stands were overflowing, and the smell of buttery popcorn filled the air.

Fans were satisfying their hunger with every type of treat the concession stand had to offer while they cheered on their favorite team.

The score was incredibly close.
It was the bottom of the 8th
when Jimmy was up to bat.

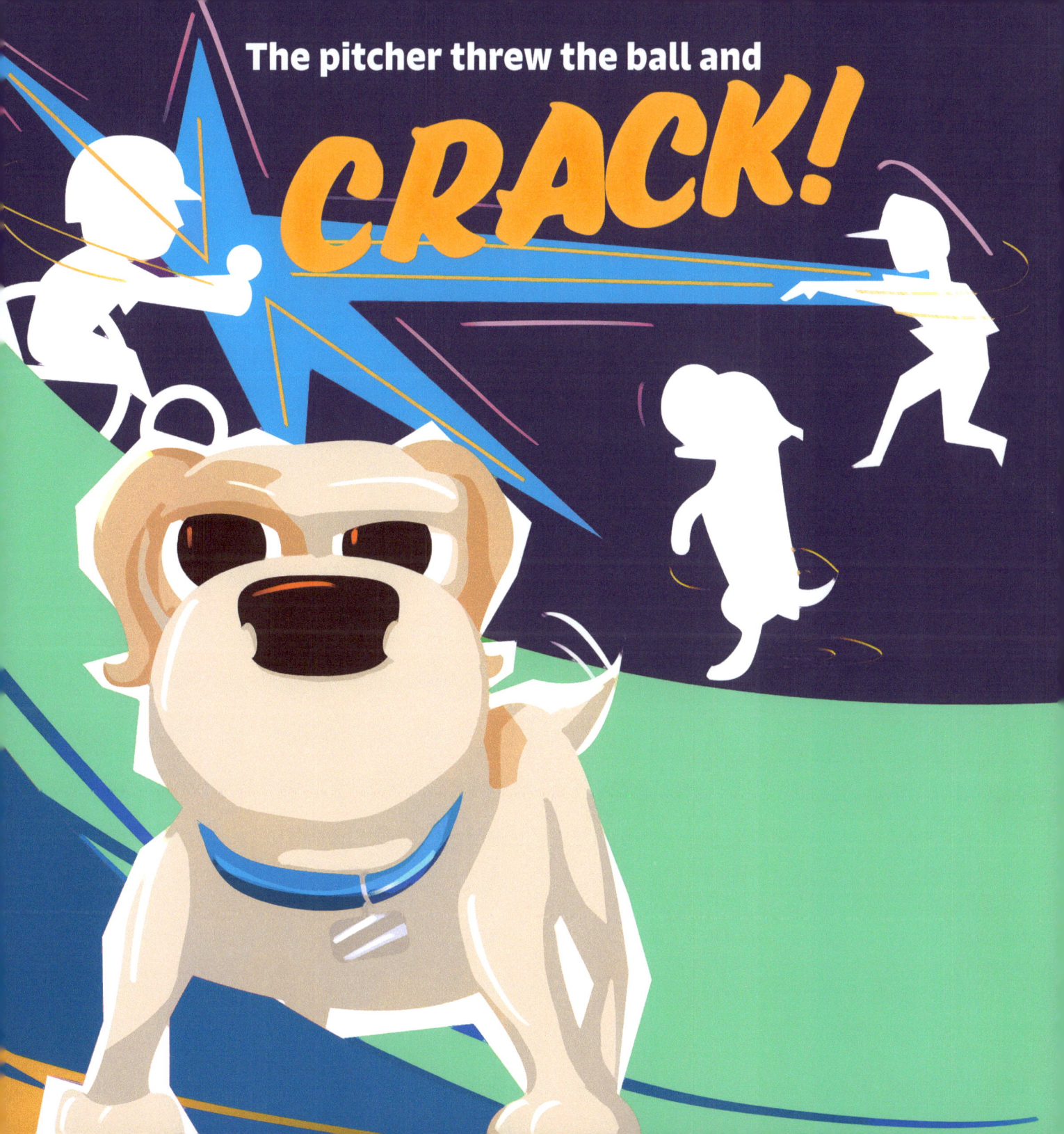

The ball flew deep into left field. Fans began to roar!

Jimmy took off toward first base and the outfielders scrambled to get to the ball.

Before they could get there, Scooter, the coach's big dog, raced onto the field.

Scooter snatched up the ball and started running around, tail wagging wildly.

A stampede of the visiting team's players raced toward Scooter.

The pitcher tried to join, but he tripped over his shoelaces and fell to the ground!

Before long, the home team and both coaches had entered the chase, too.

The crowd giggled and laughed at everyone on the field. From a distance, the whole scene looked rather silly. Two baseball teams chased a cheerful dog with a baseball in his mouth!

Scooter ran and ran all around the ball field with his drool flinging in the air.

The chase finally ended when Jimmy's little sister whistled loudly to get Scooter's attention.

Scooter paused and perked up his ears.

She called for him,
"Here, Scooter!
Wanna hot dog?!"

**Scooter immediately
dropped the slobbery ball
and ran for the food.**

Both teams agreed to call the game a tie. The ball was a dirty, drool-covered mess, and all the players were out of breath from running and laughing.

It was the silliest game anyone had ever seen!

THE END

ABOUT TJ TRUMAR

T is for Tabitha. Tabitha's favorite thing to do is *family movie night*. This is where everyone piles into the living room to watch a movie, eat popcorn, chocolate chips, and marshmallows. YES, all at once, stuff the yummy flavors in your mouth! The absolute best part is when we all get up and dance to the music at the end of the movie during the credits. You should give family movie night a try sometime!

J is for Jessica. Jessica is a goofball who loves to cuddle with her amazing husband and crazy dogs. She hopes everyone will join her in giving in to their dorky, fun side. Be silly, sing loud, dance like you know how (even when you don't), and above all, laugh - a lot! Have fun being you, because you are the only one who gets to do that!

FUN FACTS

TJ is the dynamic duo, Tabitha & Jessica. Just two gals chasing their creative dreams and sharing them with the world.

Trumar is a combination of two names, Truett and Marie – TRUMAR. This is to honor Tabitha's amazing kids and their support.

ABOUT THE ILLUSTRATOR

Patrick N. Marston works as a graphic designer and freelance illustrator. He lives in Little Rock, AR with his wife, Arielle and their two scottish terriers.

www.ingramcontent.com/pod-product-compliance
Lightning Source LLC
Chambersburg PA
CBHW041619120626
46551CB00003B/502